ESTELA AND HER FRIENDS

BY ROSIELYN P. DICO

ISBN
Hardbound-978-621-495-273-1
Softbound/Paperback-978-621-495-274-8
Mobile/Kindle-978-621-495-275-5

Published by:
Poetry Planet Book Publishing House
Rosario, Pozorrubio, Pangasinan, Philippines
Contact Number:075-6155455
Email: maritesritumalta@gmail.com

ISBN
Hardbound-978-621-495-273-1
Softbound/Paperback-978-621-495-274-8
Mobile/Kindle-978-621-495-275-5

Published by:
Poetry Planet Book Publishing House
Rosario, Pozorrubio, Pangasinan, Philippines
Contact Number:075-6155455
Email: maritesritumalta@gmail.com

PREFACE

A storybook help children develop emotional intelligence. It has the power to promote emotional and moral development. It contains numerous moments of crisis when characters make moral decisions, an important skill for children to model.

The story is about a girl who was born into a world of effortless, luxury, and never knew hardship, where her every whim was a command. She had everything in her life. She chose her friends based from their socio-economic status and ignored the poor ones.

This book will show how the girl in the story transformed her negative attitude into a positive one. This demonstrates how crucial having a true friend.

Have fun in reading.

The Author

Estella grew up in a rich family in town. Her parents were well-off, so she never experienced any hardships. She did not know about any household chores because they had helpers who did all the work at home. Estella's routine included eating, , studying, and playing online games because her parents buy everything she wants. That was her usual routine every morning.

"Auntie Wilma, please arrange the things in my bags; kindly put the mobile phone in my bag's pocket. And don't forget to prepare delicious snacks for me," Estela instructed her auntie.

"Yes, I did all the things you have said, my dear child. Everything is finished, so you may go to school already," said Wilma.

At their school, Estella always had new clothes, unlike her classmates, who wore the same clothes multiple times. Aside from the money her parents gave her every day, she always had delicious snacks whenever she went to school.

"I wish I could also taste delicious food like what Estella eats," Joy said.

"You're right Joy, Estella is very lucky because she has a lot of new clothes, while we were dressed in the old clothing of our elder sisters," said Ellen.

Her classmates look upon her with admiration, especially those who couldn't taste delicious food like she did during recess.

"Hello Joy and Ellen, what are you talking about? I don't want you to keep looking at me. You shouldn't be staring at me like that. Hmmm... You are a pain in the neck."

"You look impressive with your outfit Estella. It is a perfect fit for you. You look very lovely today."

"Yes Estella, it's true. You are beautiful. Also, I'm just curious what your snacks are because we don't even have foods like that in our house."

Hmm... Estella responded negatively in silence.

"Oh, Estella, you treat us so badly. All we want from you is friendship."

After talking to her two classmates, Estella was very annoyed and quickly left them.

Meanwhile, Estella's parents were busy with their businesses and livelihoods, so she could do things for her own pleasure. She doesn't establish friendships with her classmates who are from lower socioeconomic backgrounds.

"Estella's family is well-off. Her parents have a lot of property, unlike us, whose families are extremely poor," Joy exclaimed.

"Yes, she has everything, but her parents are always not at home because they are busy with their businesses," explained Ellen.

One morning, Estella and her mother were having a serious conversation in the living room. Her mom reminded her.

"Estela, remember to study well, because me and your father will do everything to give you a comfortable life and a good future."

"You don't need to worry about me, Mom. My academic performance is good. I never went anywhere else but home to do my projects, homework, and lesson preparation."

Estella's parents didn't provide her with much instruction due to their busy work schedules. So, Estella frequently associates with wealthy kids in school, yet she never minds her poor classmates who show genuine concern and kindness toward her.

"Ellen, I forgot my lunch at home. What should I do? I have nothing to eat for lunch, Joy said.

Ellen hesitantly suggested, "Maybe we should try asking Estella for food since she always has excess food packed every day."

"I don't want to, because she's rude. She'll surely get mad at us if we approach her. Here, let's just share my food," Joy replied without doubt.

Estella enjoyed the luxuries she was experiencing with her friends. She never thought about the classmates. Furthermore, she never pays attention to her mother's advice.

"Estella, always remember that obeying parents' advice and socializing with classmates are more important things to be proud of than materialistic things. We don't know that someday, when we have nothing, they are the people who can help us in times of need," her mother advised.

"Don't worry, Mom; my schoolmates Jackie and Anne are there for me. They were there when I enjoyed the luxuries you have given me."

"You have chosen your friends, my dear daughter. They have to be truthful and available when you need them most."

Estella merely kept playing with her phone as her mother gave her important guidance. She never gave any thought to what her mother had told her.

A week had passed, and Wilma, their helper, had to go home because her daughter was sick. It was then that Estella's mother was rushed to the hospital due to a severe illness. Estella keeps crying and pleading.

"Huhuhu, there's no one to take care of me. Where are Jackie and Anne now, I needed them to cheer me up at this very moment.

"Don't worry, Estella, we are here to comfort you. We are your true friends," Joy and Ellen said when they visited Estella.

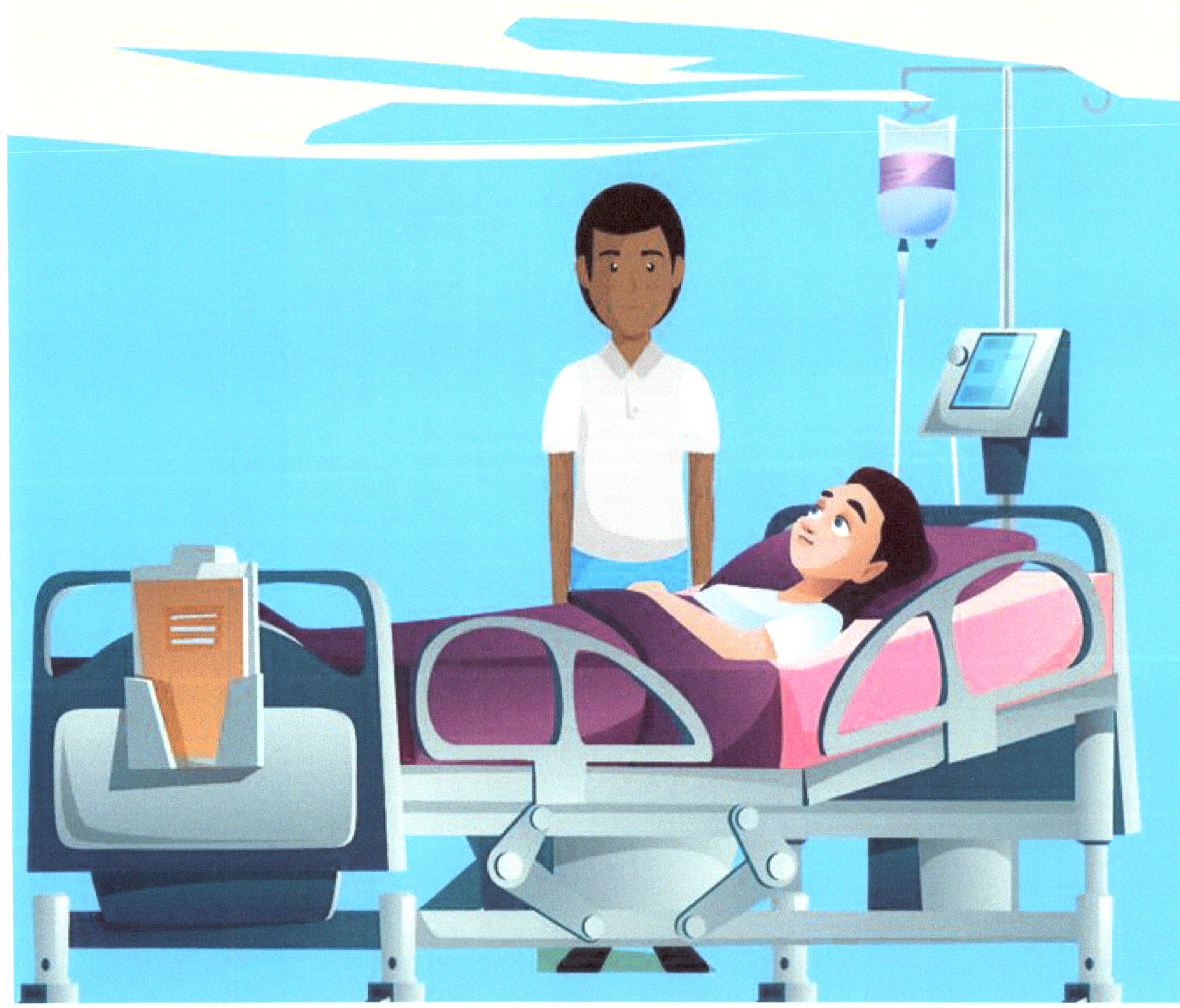

It took a long time before her mother recovered. It was at that moment that she realized the importance of having true friends. She remembered the lessons her mother had imparted to her.

"Please forgive me for my mistakes, Joy and Ellen. Now, I realized that you are good friends," Estela cried.

"Joy and Ellen, I'm sorry. I sincerely apologize for not treating you better."

"You are always welcome in our hearts, Estella. Ellen and I are here for you."

"That's true; we love you as our friend, Estella."

Every day, Estella carried the life lessons she learned from her experiences.

ABOUT THE AUTHOR

ROSIELYN P. DICO, the author, was a dedicated elementary teacher from Mangilay, Siayan, Zamboanga del Norte. She was born last March 24, 1985. She finished Bachelor in Elementary Education, major in GEN-ED, and Master of Arts in Education, major in Educational Administration at JHCSC- Dumingag Campus.

The author's journey in teaching was filled of mixed experienced. Her passion of teaching contributed much in shaping and nurturing the young minds. Yet, there were struggles encountered by the author. This personal experienced drives her commitment to help young learners.

The author was excited to share her knowledge and insights through this workbook. It's a story that it would really appeal especially the Grade -3 Learners. The whole process of writing it has been a fantastic journey of the author.

www.ingramcontent.com/pod-product-compliance
Lightning Source LLC
LaVergne TN
LVHW071224160826
845679LV00003B/902

* 9 7 8 6 2 1 4 9 5 2 7 4 8 *